The Night Before Christmas

PaRragon

Bath · New York · Singapore · Hong Kong · Cologne · Delhi
Melbourne · Amsterdam · Johannesburg · Auckland · Shenzhen

This Book Belongs To:

Andrew Soto

2011

Retold by Clement C. Moore
Illustrated by Caroline Pedler

This edition published by Parragon in 2011

Parragon Publishing
Queen Street House
4 Queen Street
Bath BA1 1HE, UK

Copyright © Parragon Books Ltd 2001

ISBN 978-1-4454-5283-8
All rights reserved
Printed in China

Twas the night before Christmas,
when all through the house
Not a creature was stirring, not even a mouse.
The stockings were hung by the chimney with care,
In hope that St. Nicholas soon would be there.

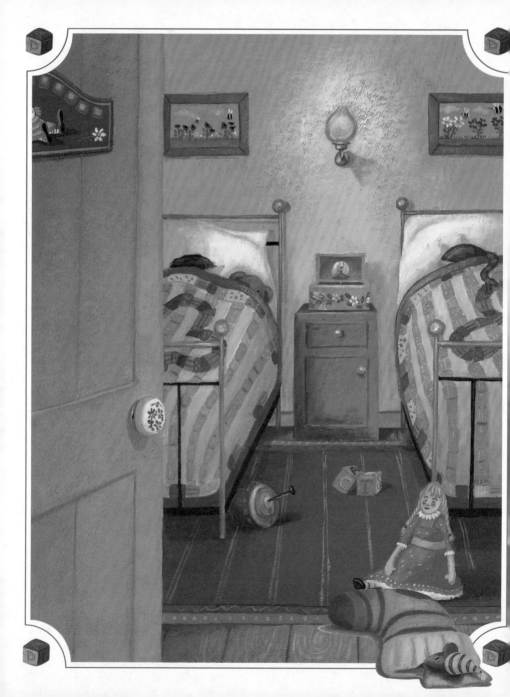

The children were nestled all snug in their beds,
While visions of sugarplums danced in their heads;
And Mama in her kerchief and I in my cap,
Had just settled down for a long winter's nap.
When out on the lawn there arose such a clatter,
I sprang from the bed to see what was the matter.

Away to the window I flew like a flash,
Tore open the shutters and threw up the sash.
The moon on the breast of the new-fallen snow
Gave lustre of midday to objects below,
When, what to my wondering eyes should appear,
But a miniature sleigh and eight tiny reindeer.

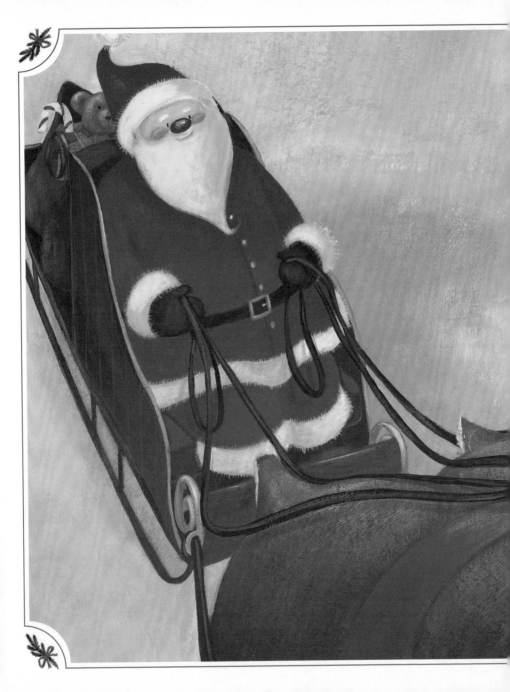

With a little old driver so lively and quick,
I knew in a moment it must be St. Nick.
More rapid than eagles his coursers they came,
And he whistled and shouted
and called them by name;

"Now Dasher! Now Dancer! Now Prancer and Vixen!
On Comet! On Cupid! On Donner and Blitzen!
To the top of the porch! To the top of the wall!
Now dash away! Dash away! Dash away all!"

As dry leaves that before the wild hurricane fly,
When they meet with an obstacle, mount to the sky,
So up to the housetop the coursers they flew,
With a sleigh full of toys and St. Nicholas too.
And then in a twinkling, I heard on the roof
The prancing and pawing of each little hoof.

As I drew in my head, and was turning around,
Down the chimney St. Nicholas came with a bound.
He was dressed all in fur, from his head to his foot,
And his clothes were all tarnished with ashes and soot.
A bundle of toys he had flung on his back,
And he looked like a pedlar just opening his pack.

His eyes — how they twinkled! His dimples — how merry!
His cheeks were like roses, his nose like a cherry!
His droll little mouth was drawn up like a bow,
And the beard of his chin was as white as the snow.

The stump of a pipe he held tight in his teeth,
And the smoke it encircled his head like a wreath.
He had a broad face and a little round belly,
That shook when he laughed, like a bowlful of jelly.

He was chubby and plump, a right jolly old elf,
And I laughed when I saw him, in spite of myself.
A wink of his eye and a twist of his head,
Soon gave me to know I had nothing to dread.

He spoke not a word, but went straight to his work,
And filled all the stockings; then turned with a jerk,
And laying his finger aside of his nose
And giving a nod, up the chimney he rose.

He sprang to his sleigh, to his team gave a whistle,
And away they all flew like the down of a thistle.
But I heard him exclaim ere he drove out of sight,
"Merry Christmas to all, and to all a goodnight!"